Oil

By Elsie Nelley

Contents

Is Oil an Important Source of Energy?

People all around the world are divided on the importance of oil. As the need for energy keeps growing, many believe oil is still one of the world's most useful resources. Others think the use of oil should be decreased and more use made of renewable resources.

an oil-fired power station

Arguments to support the use of oil

- is a most useful resource
- gives off great amounts of heat and power
- is cheaper to make than using renewable resources.

First, many people say oil is a useful source of energy because it gives off great amounts of heat and power when it burns. This makes it a good source of electricity for home and work use. It is a cheaper source of energy than renewable resources. A large amount of the world's energy is still produced in oil-fired power stations.

Arguments to support the use of oil

- is a liquid
- is easy to transport through pipelines or by oil tankers
- provides many useful by-products
- is the main source of energy in cars, etc.

These people also say oil is a useful resource because it is a liquid. It can be pumped from the ground and transported easily from one place to another through long pipelines and by large oil tankers.

They further support their beliefs by adding that processed oil provides many useful by-products that give off energy when burned. These products are the main source of energy in the engines of cars, trucks, ships, trains and planes.

Arguments against the use of oil

- supplies will run out soon
- sends carbon dioxide gas into the air
- is linked to global warming and climate change
- is unsafe to transport.

On the other hand, those who think the world's reliance on oil should be decreased say Earth's supplies of oil will run out. They also state that when oil is burnt, it sends carbon dioxide gas into the air. This gas is harmful to the environment and is linked to global warming and climate change.

Furthermore, these people say oil is easily set on fire and is unsafe to transport. Even the process of moving oil from one place to another can harm the environment.

Arguments against the use of oil

- oil spills pollute water and soil
- damages beaches and kills wildlife
- renewable resources better for the environment.

Oil tankers spill oil at sea and old pipelines can leak. Oil spills pollute water and soil. They damage beaches and kill wildlife. Many people believe these reasons are sufficient cause to invest in renewable sources of energy.

After reflecting on both sides of the argument, it would appear there are valid reasons why we must become less dependent on oil. As the need for electricity increases, renewable energy resources must be developed further. These resources can be sustained and they are also better for the environment.

The Exxon Valdez Oil Spill

On 24 March 1989, the oil tanker Exxon Valdez ran aground on a reef in Prince William Sound, Alaska. One side of the tanker was split open and huge amounts of thick crude oil spilled into the sea.

Prince William Sound

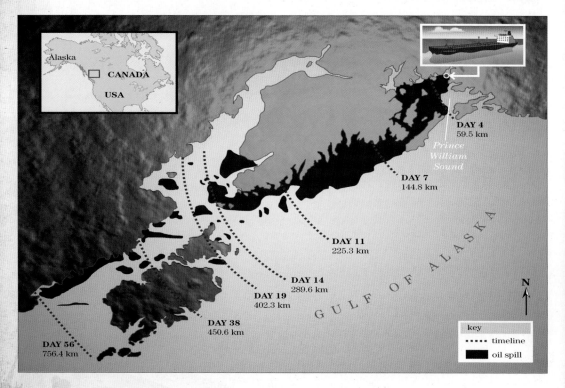

Alaska

CANADA

USA

DAY 4
59.5 km

Prince William Sound

DAY 7
144.8 km

DAY 11
225.3 km

DAY 14
289.6 km

DAY 19
402.3 km

DAY 38
450.6 km

DAY 56
756.4 km

GULF OF ALASKA

N

key
····· timeline
■ oil spill

A photograph of the Exxon Valdez run aground in 1989

Barriers were quickly placed around the oil to stop it from spreading but unfortunately, there was a huge storm in the area two days after the spill.

The storm and extremely high spring tides caused the oil to spread for great distances along the coast, onto sheltered beaches, islands, nature reserves and even up sheer rock faces. In an attempt to remove oil from the beaches, high-pressure hoses were used to spray sea water onto the oil.

Where the oil had built up in hard-to-reach places on the rocky shoreline, heated sea water was used to try to break down the pools of oil. The heated sea water removed some of the oil, but it also killed many of the tiny plants that grew on the shore and destroyed the habitats of countless sea birds and marine animals.

A fur seal is cleaned by a group of volunteers.

More than 11 000 people, including volunteers and Alaskan residents, assisted with the enormous clean-up. Some helped by rescuing birds and animals, cleaning them with soapy water or caring for them in specially set-up animal hospitals.

However, it is estimated that as many as 500 000 seabirds died because their feathers had stuck together with oil, which prevented them from swimming or flying. When they tried to clean themselves, they swallowed the oil and died.

Hundreds of otters and seals died. When the oil stuck to their fur, they were unable to keep warm. Thousands of fish are thought to have died, as well as billions of salmon and herring eggs.

Prince William Sound today

Within 12 months, there was very little visual evidence of the oil spill. However, the long-term impact on Prince William Sound and the environmental damage caused by the Exxon Valdez disaster continue to be felt today. The beauty of Prince William Sound, its importance as a fishing area and the safe habitat it provided for birds, seals, otters and other marine animals will never be the same again.